Picture Book Studio

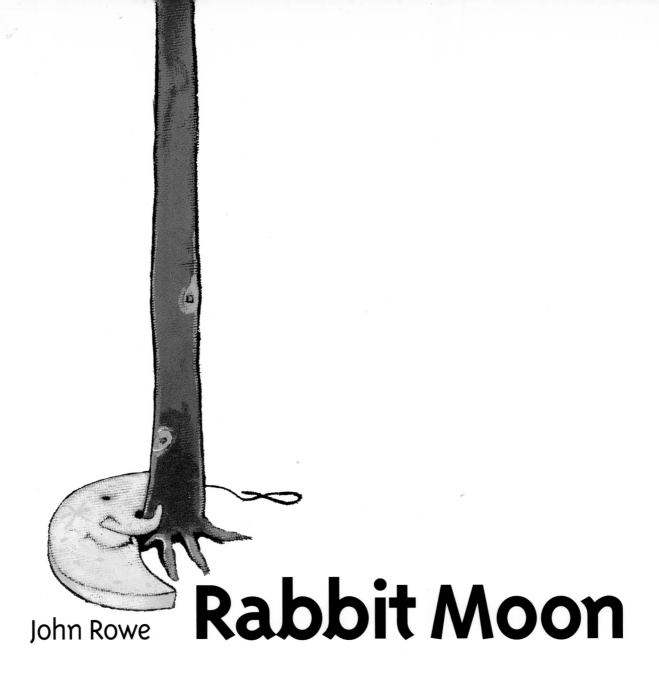

John Rowe

Rabbit Moon

Once upon a hill
there lived a rabbit named Albert.

Albert was rather old
and couldn't sleep well.
He often sat up at night
and gazed at the moon for comfort.

One night the moon wasn't there,
and this made Albert feel nervous.
He went for a walk to calm down.

Suddenly Albert spotted the moon
beside a garden wall.
"Why there you are, moon!" he called.
"You need some help!"

Albert had his friend hang the moon on the top branch of a tree.
"No, that's not nearly high enough," he said.

Next he tied the moon to a balloon. "No, that's not nearly big enough," he said.

Then he fastened the moon to a rocket.
"No, that's not nearly strong enough,"
he said.

Then he made a catapult to launch the moon, but forgot to let go of it. "Nooo, this is not nearly saaafe enough," he said.

"HELLLLLP!" he called
as he flew through the air.

"Ouch!" he shouted
as he landed in a prickly bush.
Just then the moon itself
appeared from behind a cloud.

"I did it! I did it!" he shouted.
"I saved the moon!"

Then happy old Albert
hopped slowly home in the moonlight.

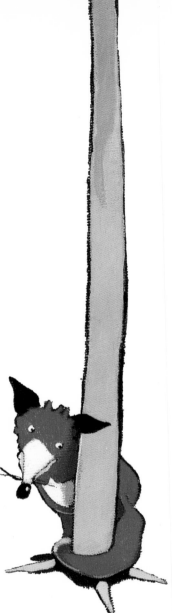

A Michael Neugebauer Book.

Copyright © 1992, Neugebauer Press, Salzburg.

Published by Picture Book Studio, Saxonville, Massachusetts.

Distributed in the United States by Simon & Schuster.

Distributed in Canada by Vanwell Publishing, St. Catharines, Ontario.

All rights reserved.

Printed in Hong Kong.

Library of Congress Cataloging in Publication Data

Rowe, John.

Rabbit moon / written and illustrated by John Rowe.

p. cm.

"A Michael Neugebauer Book"—T.p. verso.

Summary: Thinking that he has found the moon fallen from the sky,
an old rabbit tries to put it back where it belongs.

ISBN 0-88708-246-7 : $14.95

[1. Moon—Fiction. 2. Rabbits—Fiction.] I. Title.

PZ7.R7938Rab 1992

[E]—dc20 92-6047

CIP

AC

Look for this other Picture Book Studio book illustrated by John Rowe:
The Sing-Song of Old Man Kangaroo by Rudyard Kipling